MR.
CABLES

RONALD MALFI

JOURNALSTONE
YOUR LINK TO ARTIST TALENT

ISBN: 978-1-950305-52-0 (sc)
ISBN: 978-1-950305-53-7 (ebook)
Library of Congress Control Number: 2020937690

First printing edition: November 6, 2020
Published by JournalStone Publishing in the United States of America.
Cover Design and Layout: Zach McCain
Editing and Interior Layout by Scarlett R. Algee
Proofreading by Beth Renard

JournalStone Publishing
3205 Sassafras Trail
Carbondale, Illinois 62901

JournalStone books may be ordered through booksellers or by contacting:
JournalStone | www.journalstone.com

For Robbie Ribspreader, who constantly lurks just out of focus in the periphery of creation.

MR.
CABLES

1

"THIS IS THE SCARIEST book I've ever read," said the woman, placing the book on my table.

I smiled at her, as I did with everyone who queued up to have their books signed, but then I looked down at the book and my smile faltered.

It was a thick hardcover book with a creased and peeling paper dust jacket. The cover art depicted a row of homes on a suburban street, with little lampposts between each house, and was done not in great detail but in a black-and-white rudimentary fashion, like an artist's unfinished pencil sketch. The title of the book, printed in blocky yellow font, was Mr. Cables, and despite the fact that the author's name below the title was my own—Wilson S. Paventeau—I had never seen the book before.

"This isn't one of mine," I said, puzzling over the name. It was not a common one, after all. I opened the cover and flipped to the title page, already assuming this woman had printed a phony dust jacket that she'd wrapped around someone else's book, perhaps as a gag to see my reaction. Admittedly, she didn't look much like a prankster, but I'd had stranger things happen at book signings. But the title page confirmed what was printed on the dust jacket—Mr. Cables by Wilson S. Paventeau.

"I've read all your books except the latest one, and this one was by far the scariest," said the woman. She was short and squat, packaged in a gaudy paisley dress beneath a wool coat. She wrung her chubby hands together below the precipice of her overlarge bosom as she beamed at me. Her face was round, her features blunt. Her eyes were small and squinty.

"I didn't write this," I said.

The corners of the woman's small mouth sagged. "What do you mean?" Then, before I could respond, her face brightened again. She leaned closer to me. "Do you mean it's...ghostwritten?" I could smell denture cream on her breath.

"No, I mean this isn't one of my books."

She frowned. "But of course it is. It's right here."

"Yes, but—"

"There's your name on the cover."

"Yes—"

"And your..." she began, but allowed her action to finish the sentence as she turned the book over to reveal the author photo on the back.

I struggled to keep the smile on my lips. The black-and-white photo was of me, albeit an older one from earlier in my career, back when I'd sported a little more hair and a little less heft. I reopened the book, this time right to the middle, and saw that the header on the left page contained the book's title while the header on the right contained my name. A quick thumbing through the second half of the book showed that this pattern was consistent throughout the text. If it was a gag, it was an elaborate one.

From the corner of my eye, I saw the bookstore's security guard take a step in my direction. "Everything okay, Mr. Paventeau?"

"Yes, thank you," I said, and turned back to the woman wringing her hands in front of my table. The people in line behind her were beginning to peer over at us, curious. "Be honest with me," I said to the woman. "Is this a joke?"

That frown was firmly in place on the woman's face now. "A joke?"

"It's very clever. Very authentic."

"I don't understand," said the woman, a vertical crease deepening between her eyebrows.

"Did you make it yourself?" I asked.

She just stared at me. Then her round face brightened with a smile, exposing a ridge of false teeth. "You're having me on," she said, and giggled like a schoolgirl.

I managed to return her smile, though the shape of it felt like it might crack my jaw. "Where did you get this book?" I asked her.

"At a yard sale."

"Where?"

"Where?" the woman echoed. "Who can remember? It was years ago."

"I'm curious about it," I said, turning it over in my hands. "Could I borrow it? I'd pay you for it."

"For your own book?"

"What about a trade?" I suggested. "You said you haven't read my latest, right?" I tapped a palm against the stack of books at my table—the hardcover release of my latest novel, *Blood Show*.

The woman's eyebrows arched as if triggered by some mechanical device. She nodded toward the stack of books, her eyes running over the bloody font and the image of a dripping knife on the glossy dust jacket. "No, I haven't read the new one yet. That would be wonderful."

It occurred to me that this had likely been the woman's intention all along—to proffer a trade, a prank book for the real deal. And here I was, playing right into her hands. It really *was* clever. Yet this woman did not seem to be in on the prank, let alone the perpetrator. One look at the simmering confusion in her eyes told me she was as genuine as a gold coin.

"Here we are," I said, sliding a copy of *Blood Show* off the stack. I scribbled an inscription—flat-signed, not bothering to ask her name—then handed her the book.

She clutched it to her chest, her face red, her smallish mouth stretched into a grin. All confusion had been immediately eradicated from her face. I noticed that her fingernails had been gnawed down to near nonexistence, and that there was dried blood around some of the cuticles.

"You sure you won't miss it?" I said, holding up the fraudulent book.

"Oh no," she said, the smile dropping from her face. "I won't read it again. It's too scary."

"Well, enjoy the new one," I said.

"Oh, I'm sure I will. You're really just so wonderful. I'm such a huge fan. It's just...*that* one..." Her gaze skirted down to the odd book that she had given me, which was now resting in the center of the table. Something akin to distrust seemed to wash over her face. Then that jubilant smile reappeared.

Because she seemed to need some urging, I said, "Take care, now."

She gave an awkward little curtsey, then toddled across the bookstore to the exit.

2

I HAD EVERY INTENTION of waiting until I got home that evening to flip through the book, but writers are curious creatures by nature, and I wound up examining it in the food court of the mall while ingesting some orange chicken from Panda Express. I stripped the dust jacket off and saw the book's title and my name embossed in gold leaf along the spine. The date of copyright was 1999, and the publisher was Gorgon and Heavenward. I'd never heard of the publisher, and there wasn't an address or any contact information for them anywhere in the book. A quick Google search on my iPhone revealed zero results. If it was printed by a vanity press, the "publisher" wouldn't necessarily have a Web presence, or even exist beyond this very copyright page. I searched for the book's title in conjunction with my name, but none of the hits that came back had anything to do with the book.

Lastly, I turned to the back of the book, where the brief author's bio read:

> Wilson S. Paventeau is the *New York Times* bestselling author of eleven novels. He is the two-time recipient of the Bram Stoker Award®, winner of the Shirley Jackson Award, and was nominated for three Edgar Allan Poe Awards by the Mystery Writers of America. In 2010, his horror novel *Devil's Dance* was adapted into a film starring Thomas Jane and Neve Campbell. He lives in New Jersey, where he is currently at work on his next book.

It was the same bio that appeared at the back of *Blood Show*, but with one glaring difference: I was the *New York Times* bestselling author of *twelve* novels, not eleven. What made this error particularly strange was that the forgery—this *Mr. Cables*, parading as one of my own works—should have brought the tally to a baker's dozen. Instead, whoever had written and printed the book had eliminated one of my actual novels. I concluded that the forgery must have been printed prior to the release of *Blood Show*.

Of course, if the copyright date was accurate, then this book had been published in 1999, before I'd published *any* of my novels. Which was impossible.

I drove home that evening with the peculiar book sliding around on the passenger seat of my Mercedes. It was strange, but when I came to a stop at an intersection and happened to notice a large metal Dumpster in an alley between two storefronts, the urge to get out of the car and throw the book away was nearly overpowering. In fact, I'd even slipped the car into park in anticipation of climbing out, but then the traffic light changed and the guy behind me laid on his horn.

After a dinner of leftover spaghetti and a hot shower, I poured myself a glass of merlot and settled into the upholstered armchair by the bank of windows that looked out onto a vast pine forest. My nearest neighbor was over a mile away as the crow flies, but I could see a drift of smoke rising up from his chimney beyond the trees.

I opened the book and read the first sentence—

> The curious thing about Quimby was that he wasn't curious at all.

I couldn't help it; I chuckled out loud, careful not to spill my wine. If someone was attempting to emulate my style, they'd missed the essence of what the critics most often indicted me for—namely, vulgarity for vulgarity's sake. No one had ever accused me of being subtle. The opening line of *Blood Show*, for example, was:

> Blood spurted in glittery crimson ribbons as the knife was dragged across the woman's pale throat.

An opening line about someone's curiosity—or lack thereof—didn't exactly have my thumbprint on it.

I kept reading.

The book was about a man named Quimby: a fastidious, humorless bank clerk whose lack of interest and investment in the outside world manifested as an inability to achieve any level of excitement or even the simplest pleasure in life. Like an automaton, Quimby existed simply to exist, functioned only to function, and took no great satisfaction in any event, circumstance, or thought that might occur to him throughout his day. His life was tedious, repetitive, and unfettered by even the merest acquaintance, let alone a close friend or lover. His colleagues at the bank avoided him, which was Quimby's preference, and the waitress at the restaurant where he ate every day at precisely noon—the same egg salad on rye bread with a half-glass of apple juice, no ice—knew better than to engage him in conversation. There was no spark to Quimby, no passion that burned within his chest, nothing that brought a smile to his face. No creative drive or appreciation of the grand aesthetics of life.

The only measure of satisfaction Quimby received was from reading books, and even that menial task was performed not with simple pleasure but with the calculated exactitude of a surgeon excising a particularly troublesome tumor from a patient. He read not for enjoyment, in other words, but because some inexplicable compulsion drove him to do it. In fact, much of the action in the novel—if I may be so bold as to even call it "action"—came in the form of the stories Quimby read, and not necessarily with Quimby himself.

By the time I slipped a bookmark between the pages, I had read five chapters and drained two glasses of merlot. Darkness pressed against the bank of windows that overlooked the pine forest.

I turned the book over in my lap and stared at my outdated author photo on the back. Five chapters of a book where absolutely *nothing* happened in the story—arguably, there *wasn't* a story—yet I'd been so engrossed that I'd lost track of time. Exhaustion suddenly weighed on me like a change in gravity.

I set the book on the end table and was about to rise out of my chair when I noticed something about the crude artwork on the cover that I hadn't before. As described, the artwork was of a pencil drawing of a row of homes along a residential street, a lamppost stationed between each house. The artist had created the perception of darkness by etching swirls and arcs and various crosshatches of shading in the spaces between and above the houses. The thing I noticed now—the thing I hadn't seen until that very moment—was that the artist had also sketched the suggestion of a figure among the crosshatching. A cursory glance might allow the figure to go unnoticed—and indeed it had with me, until now—but the more I stared at it, the more those variants of shading in the pencilwork conspired to create the vestige of a slender man standing between two of the houses, and partially obscured by a lamppost.

"Hello there," I said, and ran my thumb across the figure, as if to smudge it out of existence. But of course the figure remained. And the longer my gaze lingered on it, the more it seemed to retreat back into the shadows and into nonexistence again.

It was exhaustion. My eyes burned with it.

I went to bed, and I won't lie: I dreamed about the lackluster Quimby.

3

THE NEXT DAY, I phoned my agent.

"You should be honored," she said. "They say emulation is the highest form of flattery."

"It's not emulation or even plagiarism. They're just using my name."

"Yeah, there was a guy who uploaded a bunch of lousy ebooks on Amazon under the name 'Stephen King,' I think. Wound up making some bank, too. It's become something of a trend."

"This book was published in 1999. Or at least that's what the copyright says, although that can't be true. Either way, it doesn't exist on Amazon, or anywhere else, for that matter."

"Not on eBay?"

"Nowhere. According to the Internet, the book doesn't exist. Neither does the publisher."

"Who's the publisher?"

"Gorgon and Heavenward. Ever heard of them?"

"No, but that doesn't mean anything."

"I went to the U.S. Copyright Office's website but couldn't find a listing. Which means the copyright is bogus, too."

"Hmmm," she said.

"I thought it might be a vanity press," I suggested.

"Is there a chance the person might just actually have the same name as you?"

"I went down that alley, too. I found a Wilson *Parenteau* on Facebook, believe it or not, but no other *Paventeau*. None in the White

Pages online or anywhere on Google. Besides, Susan, they used my author photo and bio. The photo's an old one and the bio isn't one hundred percent accurate, but they're mine."

"That's really bizarre, Wil. Do you want to send me the book?"

"I want to finish it first."

My agent laughed. "You're *reading* it?"

"Bested by curiosity, I guess," I said, and the first sentence from the novel rose up in my mind—how the curious thing about Quimby was that he wasn't curious.

"Is it any good?"

"You know, I can't really tell. If I explained it to you, you'd probably fall asleep. I mean, I've read maybe fifty pages and absolutely nothing has happened yet. But there's just something about it that I can't explain. Even weirder is that the woman who gave it to me said it was the scariest thing I've ever written, yet I'm not even sure it's a horror novel. I'm not sure *what* kind of novel it is. It's about as scary as milk."

"Heck, maybe it's got a killer twist ending. If it's any good, we can turn around and option it to Hollywood. It's already got your name on it."

It was a joke, of course, but for some reason the comment made me uncomfortable. "Maybe," I said.

We discussed other matters, and by the time we hung up, I found myself anxious to get back to the novel. I'd left it on the table beside the armchair in the living room last night, and it was still there now, framed in a rectangle of daylight coming through the floor-to-ceiling window. I poured a mug of coffee, then settled down in the armchair, promising myself I'd read for only a half hour before heading to my den to get some work done.

The story was still as uneventful as it had been the night before. In fact, I was halfway through the book before the titular Mr. Cables made his appearance, and even that turned out to be a disappointment: Mr. Cables was nothing more than the main character in one of the books Quimby was reading. Much of chapter seven was devoted to the ominous Mr. Cables, who spent his days inexplicably traveling on city buses and watching random commuters while scribbling notes (presumably about them) in a small memo pad. In the evenings he combed through stacks of books for the answer to some unknown question. It was at this point that

I realized I was reading a book about a man reading a book about a man reading a book.

When I paused in my reading to refresh my coffee, I realized I'd spent three hours in the armchair with the book. I stood there, staring at the brass clock on the mantel and at the panels of sunlight that had repositioned themselves across the living room, and tried to account for what had kept me so enraptured with the book. But I could make no sense of it.

The front door opened, and Trudy Parrott's cheery voice crooned a spirited *halloooo* down the hallway. A moment later, she appeared in the kitchen doorway, looking like an Eskimo in her winter hat and coat, her face red from the cold.

"Good afternoon, Mr. Paventeau," she said, tugging off her big fuzzy mittens.

I'd forgotten it was Trudy's day to clean the house. I tied my bathrobe closed and offered her a cup of coffee.

"I've already had my one cup for the day. If I drink more than that, I'll be up half the night with the shimmies. How did the book signing go yesterday?"

"Very well. It was nice."

"Is that the last of them?"

"For the winter, yes."

"It's good to be home, isn't it?"

"It really is, Trudy."

I went to the coffeepot, refilled my mug, then told my housekeeper that I would be in the den for the rest of the day getting some work done.

My den was situated in the part of the house I thought of as the Quiet Corner. There was only one window and the view was of the dense firs, so there wasn't much to compete with my concentration except the occasional squirrel. I'd written seven of my twelve books in this room, and although the entry into each one of those stories was different, the process had always been the same. The mind was allowed to run free while the hands were put to the keys and forced to labor.

I got very little work done that day, however. It took me the better part of an hour to string together a few sentences, and even then I wasn't exactly sure what those sentences were supposed to say. My mind was on the mysterious book, which I had left on the end table beside the armchair in the living room. I considered going to retrieve it, but the thought of my housekeeper catching me in the act filled me with a measure of inexplicable shame, as if there was something downright perverse about my association with that mysterious text. I decided that was my subconscious telling me I needed to focus on my own writing, but I knew that was a lost cause at the moment—the old word-maker in my head had shuddered and gone to sleep for the afternoon.

I spent the rest of the afternoon making phone calls to several used and rare bookstores. None of the shops that I called had ever heard of a novel titled *Mr. Cables*, though one shop owner said he had a collection of Wilson S. Paventeau first editions, and he'd be more than happy to have me come in and sign them. Moreover, no one had ever heard of a publisher called Gorgon and Heavenward. This convinced me it was a one-off vanity printing and nothing more, though why the true author had used my name, photo, and bio, I still had no idea. By the time I got off the phone, I was not only exhausted; I was defeated.

There was a couch in my den, and it wasn't unusual for me to make good use of it after a strenuous afternoon of writing. The writing hadn't been strenuous, of course—it had been nonexistent, for all intents and purposes—but my fatigue was so great that I decided to grant myself maybe forty-five minutes of shuteye before attempting to rouse the word-maker and get back to work. I kicked off my slippers, reclined on the sofa, and laced my hands behind my head. With my eyes closed, I listened to the sound of Trudy's vacuum moving up and down the hall, lulling me toward sleep.

4

WHEN I AWOKE, DUSK had turned the sky outside the den window into a palette of deepening pastels. I'd wasted a whole day.

"Crap."

I sat up, rubbed my face, then kicked my feet back into my slippers. The sound of Trudy's vacuum cleaner sounded like it was right outside the door. She should have been gone by now—she hated driving at night, particularly along the winding, forested driveway that led down the hill from my house to the main road—and it would be fully dark soon.

I opened the door to my den to find the vacuum cleaner roaring in the middle of the hall, the hose attachment leaning against the wall unattended.

"Trudy?" I called over the vacuum's roar. I went down the hall and pulled the plug; the vacuum whined as it died. "Trudy?"

No answer.

Trudy was in her late sixties and was maybe eighty pounds overweight. As I hurried down the hall, I feared I'd find her sprawled out on the living room floor, dead of a heart attack, her eyes swollen in their sockets, her spittle-flecked face like gray marble. My own heart was thudding like mad by the time I turned the corner and came into the living room.

Trudy was sitting in my armchair, that peculiar novel opened up in her lap. She was studying one of the pages with the intensity of someone engaged in prayer while gnawing ravenously at her thumbnail.

"Trudy," I said. And when she didn't look up—when she didn't respond at all—I put a little more force behind it: "Trudy!"

My housekeeper looked up, startled. "Oh," she said, popping her thumb from her mouth; I noticed a bead of blood around the cuticle. "Oh..." She glanced back down at the book, then back up at me. While I was relieved that she hadn't died on my floor, the expression on her face didn't fill me with confidence that she was in perfect health: She had been red-faced from the cold when she'd arrived hours earlier, but now her face was pale, her eyes wide as flashbulbs. She stood up from the chair sharply, knocking the book to the floor.

"Are you okay?" I asked, picking the book up off the floor.

She glanced around the room, as if searching for something.

"What's wrong?" I said.

"I guess I lost track of time, Mr. Paventeau. I haven't cleaned in here. I...I haven't cleaned anywhere." She blinked her overlarge eyes, clearly bewildered. "I'm sorry. I don't know what..."

I set the book on the end table, and when I looked up, I saw that Trudy was staring at it.

"I saw the book," she said, "and didn't recognize it. You know I've read all your books, Mr. Paventeau, or at least I *thought* I had—"

"It isn't mine," I said.

"—so I thought I'd just read the first page," Trudy went on, not hearing me. "Just the first page. But then I guess I got lost in it, and lost track of time, and, Mr. Paventeau, I apologize, I can come back tomorrow and do the work I should have done today. I'm so embarrassed."

"It's okay," I said. "Are *you* okay? You seem shaken up."

"That book," she said, still staring at it.

"What about it?"

"It's..." She looked at me. "Can I speak candidly, Mr. Paventeau?"

"Of course."

"You know I just *adore* your work, and really, I'm no critic, what do I know? It's just that..."

"What, Trudy? What is it?"

"It's *horrible.*" She brought a hand up to her mouth, as if her own words had startled her.

"In what way?" I asked.

"In *every* way. It's not like your regular books. This one is...it's just *awful.* I feel so terrible saying that, Mr. Paventeau, but it's *awful.*"

It was clear that she didn't mean it was boring or silly or trite or just poorly written; by *awful,* she meant it had scared the daylights out of her. She all but trembled as she stood there, and her gaze kept sliding back to the book on the end table, as though it were calling to her. She looked at it the way someone might eyeball a rattlesnake to make sure it wasn't creeping any closer through the underbrush.

"What exactly did you find so unappealing about the book?" I asked her. "Can you explain it to me?"

Her mouth opened, and I waited for some explanation, some critique, a statement of any kind that might lend some clarity to this mystery...but then she glanced out the windows at the darkening pine forest and at the purple-orange light draining quickly from the sky.

"I should leave," she said. "It'll be dark soon."

"I can drive you."

"No, Mr. Paventeau. I've wasted enough of your time today, sitting and reading when I should have been working. No, no. I'll be back tomorrow to make things right."

"That isn't necessary—"

"It is. I have a job to do and I mean to do it. Goodnight, Mr. Paventeau. Goodnight."

She hurried down the hall while tugging her coat on. She only had one arm in a sleeve when she went out the front door. I got the impression that, for whatever reason, she didn't want to spend another second in the house.

It's not the house, I thought. *It's the book. She's frightened of it. Not just of the story, but of the book itself.*

I turned back to the book on the end table. "Scared her pretty good, didn't you?" Although for the life of me, I couldn't figure out *why.*

I picked it up off the end table, and for a moment I was filled with the compulsion to take it straight out to the trash. To throw it away and not worry about it a second longer. But then the compulsion faded, and instead I took the book into my den. I fired up my scanner and copied the first eighty or so pages of the novel. I sent the file to my email, then logged into my email account and forwarded the pages to my agent, with a quick note asking her to give them a read and tell me her thoughts.

When I was done, I turned the lights off in the den and was about to head back into the hall when I saw someone standing outside the window, staring in at me. The sight startled me and I nearly dropped the book. I closed the lid of my laptop, eliminating the last source of light in the room, so that it was brighter outside in the moonlight than it was inside the den. But it was still too dark out there to make out any details.

Logic told me it was Trudy, having forgotten something…but what logic failed to supply was why Trudy would be peeping in the den window at me instead of coming back into the house.

Because she doesn't want to come back into the house. Because she's afraid.

I hurried down the hall and went out the front door. Trudy's car was no longer parked outside, but by this point I had dismissed the notion that it had been my housekeeper staring at me from the other side of the window.

The den's solitary window was around the side of the house, and faced the northern slope of the pine forest. There was no one there, though this didn't help ease my nerves. I stood motionless—even held my breath—while listening for sounds that might betray the location of the trespasser. But the surrounding forest was silent. This close to winter, even the birds and the crickets were gone.

I glanced down and saw I was still clutching that mysterious, inexplicable book in my hands. The trashcans were lined up against the side of the house, and on impulse, I tossed *Mr. Cables* into the nearest bin.

"To hell with it," I muttered, suddenly aware of the cold. I hurried back inside, bolted the door, then took a shower.

5

IT WAS TWO DAYS later when I received the phone call from my agent. I had written ten pages and was feeling pretty good about the new novel I was working on, so when I recognized my agent's phone number on the caller ID, I answered cheerily.

"I read it," she said, her voice flat, "and I'm not sure what to say about it."

For a moment, I thought she was talking about the new manuscript I was working on, and I tried to remember if I'd sent her an early draft of the first couple of chapters. "What exactly did you read?" I queried.

"Those pages you sent me two nights ago," she said. "The ones from that book."

It was like being struck openhanded across the face. Over the past two days I'd become so engrossed in my work that I'd forgotten all about the peculiar novel with my name on the cover, to include the fact that I'd emailed my agent a bunch of pages from it.

"Oh," I said, suddenly feeling cold. I gazed out the wall of windows and could see my neighbor's chimney unspooling a gray runner of smoke into the bright, cloudless blue sky. "What did you think?"

"Well, it's unsettling," she said. She made no effort to mask the distaste in her voice. "To be honest, it's been bothering me ever since I read it."

"I don't understand," I said. "It's boring, I'll say that much, but I fail to see what's so unsettling or frightening about the book."

"Haven't you *read* it?"

"Half of it," I said, recalling that it was still outside in my trashcan, where I'd tossed it two nights ago.

"For starters," she said, "the language is...I don't know how to describe it...the language is just *off*. It's almost as if it was a bad translation, or written by someone whose first language isn't English. Did you notice the unusual phrasing? The way many of the sentences have different and sometimes even contradictory meanings the more you read them?"

"No," I said. "I didn't notice any of that."

"But it's not just a poor translation or bad writing. In fact, I think it's just the opposite—I think the writing is so deliberate and precise that it tricks you into missing some of the meaning behind the words. You have to read some sentences two or three times to actually catch the meaning."

I was shaking my head, confused. "This is news to me," I said.

"And it's not done just to be clever," my agent went on. "I mean, it sounds paranoid, but I kept getting the impression that the way the sentences were structured was to hide some malicious intent buried in the words. Like there's something nefarious buried in there. Does that make any sense?"

"No," I told her. "None at all."

"Take another look at the structure of the sentences, the paragraphs. Pick a particular paragraph and read it over to yourself, three or four times. Out loud, even. See what you come away with."

"All right," I said, not bothering to explain that the book was currently taking up residence with some empty Michelob bottles and old Chinese food containers.

"It's completely unapproachable, and although I can't explain why, I get the sense that it's actually deliberate. It's almost as if it doesn't want to be read. Not by me, anyway."

"That's pretty deep."

"And then there's the story itself," she went on. "The protagonist—"

"Quimby," I said.

"Yes. Listen, I've read some gruesome manuscripts before—and I'm including your work in this category, Wilson—"

"Jeez, thanks."

"—but the stuff described here is just...I don't know. It's like the difference between watching a violent slasher film and one of those videos of terrorists cutting people's heads off."

"What are you talking about? Susan, I didn't read a single thing in that book that's half as violent as an old Road Runner cartoon. Are we talking about the same thing here?"

"I don't know how you could miss it," she said. "And it's not *violence*—I don't mean that—but it's more of this...this very palpable dread. Whenever Quimby rides the bus and watches those people, and then he gets off and follows them to—"

"No, no, you're wrong," I said. "Quimby doesn't ride the bus. Mr. Cables rides the bus. Quimby just reads about Mr. Cables riding the bus, and even then there's nothing that actually happens."

"No, Wilson, *you're* the one who's wrong. Mr. Cables *is* Quimby. Those aren't books he's *reading*, those are things he's *writing* about the people he's following."

I opened my mouth to say something, but found that my mind was blank. I didn't know how to respond. Of course my agent was incorrect in her assessment...yet there was a part of me that realized she was *right*, too, and that I had somehow missed this huge detail among the mundane passages of that strange little novel. That Quimby was actually Mr. Cables made complete sense to me—it was like a puzzle piece snapping into place in the center of my head—yet it did nothing to explain the plot of the story. It explained nothing. The puzzle was still incomplete.

I was reading the book wrong, I thought to myself, the phone growing hot against the side of my face. *I do this for a goddamn living, yet I was reading the book wrong. How is that possible?*

"One last thing," my agent said. "The pages are misnumbered."

"What?"

"I thought you had skipped some pages when you sent me the file—I'm missing pages thirty-three through forty-one—but there was no hiccup in the flow of the text, no break in continuity. So my guess is the page numbers in the book itself are incorrect."

This was something I hadn't noticed, either. I suddenly felt like a fool.

"I'll have to check," I muttered into the receiver. "In the meantime, I'll send you some more pages—"

"No." My agent's voice was as sharp as a knife blade. "No, Wilson, I don't want to read anymore."

"Come on, Susan, it couldn't have messed you up that badly."

"I didn't think so, until I had some of the worst nightmares of my life last night. I mean, I felt like I was eight years old again. It's just what I said—like it doesn't *want* to be read, and it's scaring me off, giving off a stink like a skunk to keep me away." She laughed—a nervous titter void of humor. "It's nuts, right? But no thanks. Enough is enough for me. However," she added, an uptick in her tone, "I took the liberty of contacting someone I know who runs an old book emporium in the city. I told him about the book and he seemed interested in looking at it. You'll have to come into the city, of course, but it might help shed some light on who published the thing."

"Yeah, okay."

She gave me a Manhattan address, which I jotted on a napkin, and then she said, "Guy's name is Finter, Ross Finter. If anyone can give you some insight into that book, it's him."

"Thanks, Susan."

"How's the new novel coming?"

"Wonderful."

"Send some pages my way? I'm heading to Montauk with the in-laws and could use an excuse to hide in the guest room for a few hours."

"Sure. I'll send you something later today."

"All right." And then there was a pause, as if she wanted to say something more but couldn't quite summon the words. For whatever reason, I convinced myself that had she spoken, it would have been some sort of warning, although a warning about what, I had no idea. The book? What could be dangerous about a book?

A memory flickered to life inside me—or, more accurately, the ghost-words from my former self, orating before a classroom of college freshmen in a time before my first novel was published, saying something akin to all honest books are also dangerous books, which makes all honest writers dangerous writers. Fortunately for the unguarded populace, there were few honest writers. And the students would laugh. I hadn't thought about my days in front of the classroom in several years, and even now the idea of it glimmered with an oily patina, like some old clunky relic polished to a desperate shine.

"Look, I gotta go," she said, the old chipper quality back in her voice. "You take care. And go see Finter."

"Right," I said, and hung up. I was just about to place the portable phone on the cradle when it rang in my hand. "Susan?"

"Mr. Paventeau…" It was my housekeeper, her voice noticeably unsteady. "It's Trudy Parrott. I want to apologize for not showing up yesterday."

"You weren't scheduled for yesterday, Trudy."

"I said I would come and make up for the work I didn't do the day before—"

"It's not necessary."

"—but I just couldn't do it. I couldn't do it, Mr. Paventeau. I'm sorry."

"Trudy, what's wrong? You sound upset."

"It's that *book*, Mr. Paventeau. I just can't stop thinking about it. And the *nightmares*! I'm terrified of it."

"Don't be silly. It's just a book."

"Is it? Is it really?"

Not sure how to respond, I cleared my throat and said, "I've gotten rid of it. I've thrown it out. So…"

"I'm not sure that matters."

"Trudy, please, you're making me feel terrible. Over a *book*? What can I do to make you feel better?"

"There's nothing you can do. I think it's best we go our separate ways."

"This is silly."

"Not to me. Not to me."

"Trudy—"

"Goodbye, Mr. Paventeau." And before I could utter another word, Trudy Parrott hung up.

6

OF COURSE, I WAS compelled to dig the book out of the trash and take it back inside. After my conversation with my agent, how could I not? I couldn't fathom how she was able to come away with such a vastly different reading experience, and I was desperate to study the pages more closely to see what it was that I'd initially missed. But before I set myself to reading, I flipped to page thirty-three...only to discover that there *was* no page thirty-three. Just as my agent had informed me, the pages jumped from thirty-two to forty-three. Yet the sentence on the bottom of page thirty-two continued onto page forty-three without missing a beat. My agent had been right: The book was numbered incorrectly.

I ran with Susan's suggestion and read several passages out loud. But despite this recommendation, I came away no wiser to whatever nefariousness my agent was worried might be buried within the text. This wasn't a goddamn spell book, for Christ's sake. And after ten minutes of reciting passages from the book to my reflection in the hallway mirror, I began to feel like a fool and called it quits.

I knew I shouldn't waste any more time with the book, but when I sat down to put my own words to paper (or, more precisely, onto a computer screen), I found the word-maker in my head had gone dormant again. It was as if the novel with my name on the cover was a talisman keeping my muse at bay—a physical manifestation of Mr. Cables, whose cold, pitiless stare had cast my muse into hiding. So instead of writing, I fired off my most recent pages to my agent, then retired to the living room where, reclining in the armchair, I continued reading the strange novel.

The next time I looked up from the page, it was dark outside again. This stunned me; it felt like I had only been reading for twenty or thirty minutes. But when I consulted the clock on the fireplace mantel, I saw that four hours had sped by. I glanced back down at the book in my lap and saw that I only had about a dozen or so pages left to go before I finished it, which only made me want to read on and get it over with. Finishing the lousy thing might serve to free me from its grasp, allowing me to get on with my life. Yet at the same time I was unnerved by the prospect of slipping back into Quimby's mundane little world, for fear that even more time would slip by me unnoticed. I had this vision of closing the book after I'd finished reading, only to look over at my reflection in one of the large floor-to-ceiling windows and find that I'd become an old man. It was laughable...but the fear of it was enough for me to set the book aside for the night.

In the kitchen, I noticed the napkin on the counter on which I'd jotted down the address and phone number of a book dealer in Manhattan named Finter. I picked up the phone and dialed the number, waited, waited. It never rang. I hung up the phone and then tried again, but this time there was no dial tone—just the dim hum of distant static.

"Wonderful."

I replaced the receiver on the cradle, then stood there with my hands on my hips, for some reason feeling like a stranger in my skin. I was thinking again of my days teaching English and creative writing at Montclair Community College, though this time those thoughts surfaced because of the pages I'd read. Having exhausted all the books in his personal collection and in the local library, Quimby had gone to the local college to scour the library shelves. On this occasion he'd dressed in a wide-brimmed fedora and a trench coat, which was the same attire the character Mr. Cables wore when riding the bus and scribbling his cryptic notes in his memo pad—the only similarity between the two characters that I was able to discern during the hours I'd just spent reading. How my agent was able to figure out that Mr. Cables was Quimby's alternate personality was beyond me.

That isn't what she said, I quickly corrected myself, my gaze returning inevitably back to the book on the table beside the armchair. *She never said Mr. Cables was Quimby's alternate personality. She said they were the same* person, and maybe that means something different than someone having an alternate personality. As if they're the same person while simultaneously being two separate and distinct people.

I realized that my thoughts were no longer making sense. This whole Mr. Cables thing had spun me for a loop, and it was occupying too much of my time. I needed to clear it from my head.

Because the urge to keep reading the book was too great—an urge to which I did not wish to succumb—I returned to my den, not to write, but to hunt around for an altogether different text among my myriad bookshelves. My stuff was in good order, and I was able to locate it with little difficulty.

It was the yearbook from Montclair Community College, graduation year 2000—my last year as a teacher before I began writing full time. It was the year my first novel, The Body Fields, was published. The advance hadn't been huge, but translation rights had sold to twenty-four countries, and there was a sizable film option from a major studio on the heels of publication. I finished out the school year, then quit and never looked back.

I'm looking back now, I told myself, sitting cross-legged on the floor with the yearbook opened up in my lap. I'm creeping back down memory lane, aren't I? And for what reason? Why am I back here, after all these years? What ghosts do I expect to find?

I didn't know what ghosts I expected to find, but I knew why I had returned and why I was now thumbing through the pages of this old yearbook. In the novel, there was no name given to the college that Quimby visits, but its similarities to Montclair Community, right down to the green-and-gold school colors and the whippoorwill mascot, couldn't be denied. The description of the quaint residential street that bordered the northernmost part of the campus in the novel matched my recollection of Primrose Avenue, the quaint residential street that bordered the northernmost part of the real Montclair's campus. The street where I'd lived while teaching at the school.

It was silly, of course. I was filling in the descriptive gaps with my own memories, knowledge, and life experiences, just like any other reader, nothing more than that—

But then there it was, laid out before me, the yearbook photograph taking up both pages so that the crease ran down the center of Primrose Avenue, that picturesque little boulevard on the outskirts of Montclair

Community College, with its tidy row of identical homes, a lamppost between each house—

I snapped the yearbook shut. Sweat had oozed from my pores and was trickling down my forehead, stinging my eyes. I could taste my heartbeat at the back of my throat.

I had always been amazed at a boardwalk artist's ability to capture the likeness of a person in just a few simple, well-placed lines. Comparing the photograph of Primrose Avenue in the yearbook to the rudimentary sketch of houses on the dust jacket of *Mr. Cables* was no different. I knew without a doubt that the drawing was a reproduction of the street that bordered the college where I used to teach, now almost twenty years ago.

Impossible? It *was*...unless the person who'd fabricated the novel had done so with the intention of tormenting me...that if they'd done their homework, they would have eventually come to know that I had taught classes at Montclair Community College, that I had mentioned it on occasion in interviews, that...

But *why*? Why would someone go through the effort? Particularly if they couldn't ensure that the book would ultimately wind up in my hands. That round-faced woman at the book signing said she'd picked up the novel years ago at a garage sale. Was she lying? Was she the pivotal character in this sinister plot against me?

I laughed aloud, knowing that if I didn't release some pressure, the entire framework of my mental stability might break apart at the seams. I slid the yearbook back into its accustomed slot on the bookshelf. Trembling—I won't deny it—I got up, went back down the hall, and picked the book up off the end table.

Throw it away for good this time.

Trash collection was tomorrow morning. All I'd have to do was dump it in a trash bag and drive it down to the curb. Simple as pie. And as I held that book and looked at its cover, knowing damn well that the drawing was a reproduction of that real-life street, I had every intention of doing just that.

But instead, I wound up sitting back down in the armchair and reading the rest of the book, straight to the end.

7

EVERY TIME I VISITED Manhattan, I felt the tendrils of my childhood agoraphobia tighten like a straitjacket around my body. It wasn't so much a fear of open space as it was a strident and escalating discomfiture upon being infused in that tidal crowd of people, one bobbing cork on a sea of bobbing corks, with no means of extraction—of salvation—in sight.

Finter's Used Books was a tiny storefront on Worth Street, incongruously situated in the city's financial district. Had it been a luncheonette or a bank or a bar, it might have thrived; but the tattered cloth awning and cracked front windows expressed just how neglected and unprofitable this out-of-place business was.

The copy of *Mr. Cables* tucked under one arm and wrapped in a plastic bag, I stepped into the tiny store. A bell tinkled overhead—a charming if useless flourish. The bookstore was basically a narrow passageway whose walls were overflowing with thick, musty volumes. My agent had called the place an emporium, but this was nothing more than the corridor of a submarine. My agoraphobia was replaced with claustrophobia, and I undid the top button of my shirt and tugged at the collar of the undershirt beneath.

There was a small desk cluttered with books framed in the daylight of the front window, but there was no one in the place. It even *smelled* unused; I imagined this must be what it's like to crack open a pharaoh's tomb.

I said, "Hello?" and my voice became the opposite of an echo: The sound seemed to thud dully in the air directly in front of my face and fall to the scuffed linoleum floor, dead as a bird that had struck a window.

Nonetheless, it did the trick—a frazzled, gnomish gentleman in a tweed vest and sleeve garters peered around a shelf of books toward the rear of the shop. He scowled at me, then hustled an armload of paperbacks toward the front of the store, where he allowed them to tumble onto the sunlit desk.

"Can I help you?" His tone suggested he was well aware of the store's lack of patronage, and found my arrival not only inopportune but suspicious.

"Are you Mr. Finter?"

His wizened old eyes narrowed, the suspicion increasing. "Yessss," he said, drawing out the word the way a cartoon snake might.

I explained who I was, how I'd gotten his name, and how I'd attempted to call several times before coming out here, but that his phone seemed to be disconnected. Before I could get into the reason for my visit, he scooped up the telephone receiver from beneath the desk and pressed it to one ear.

"Sounds fine to me," he said, as if catching me in a lie. He buried the receiver back beneath the desk, then, in a lower voice, muttered, "What is it you want, Mr. Paventeau?"

I explained how a woman at a book signing had given me the strange book with my name on it—a book I hadn't written. I told him that my efforts to locate any information about the publisher were futile, and that I was hoping he could provide me with some answers.

"Let's see it," he groused, tugging a pair of wire-rimmed glasses from the breast pocket of his vest.

I took the book out of the plastic bag and set it down on the desk. It occurred to me that this old, tattered hardcover looked perfectly at home in this bookshop, a relic within a relic, a ghost inside a ghost. At that moment, I realized just how much I wanted to be rid of it.

Finter picked up the book, turned it over in his hands, opened the cover...sniffed the pages within. He ran one crooked finger along the embossed spine. "This is hand-stitched. A nice piece of work."

"That right?"

"Gorgon and Heavenward," he muttered, opening the front cover and gazing down at the copyright page.

"Ever heard of them?"

"No. They don't exist."

"They don't?"

He flipped to the bio, read it, then stared up at me. His eyes were magnified behind the lenses of his glasses. "Is this your biography?"

"It is, but it's incorrect. I've written twelve books. This bio says I've only written eleven."

"Which book is missing?"

"I don't know," I said.

Finter's gaze flitted up at me. He stared over the rimless lenses of his spectacles at me, studying my face as if to determine whether or not I'd just spoken the truth. "Are you sure?" he pressed.

"I don't know," I repeated. "How am I supposed to know?"

Evidently satisfied with my answer, he turned back to the front of the book, studied the copyright page again, the title page, searching.

"There's no card page, if that's what you're looking for," I said, referring to the page that lists all the other works by the author, typically located just before the title page. Had there been one, the missing book would have been obvious. "I've already checked."

"Yes, I see that."

"Also, there's this," I said, flipping to the end of the book. I turned toward the last page of the story and pointed to the bottom, where the sentence ended abruptly, unfinished.

"There's no page missing?" Finter asked.

"There must be, because a book usually doesn't end in the middle of a sentence like that." The book had concluded with Mr. Cables, the last remaining commuter on a city bus, meticulously printing in one of his memo pads. The bus stopped at an intersection, the doors hissed open...but then the story had ended in mid-sentence.

Finter grunted like an animal, then proceeded to unwrap the dust jacket from the book. Dust particles took flight and swirled about in the sunlight coming through the window. Finter gave a cursory glance at the book's spine again before setting the volume down on the desk and turning his attention to the dust jacket. As he studied it, he said, "Is it any good?"

"The book? It's pretty boring, actually. Nothing happens. I'm not sure I even understand it. But..." And here I let my voice die.

He looked up at me over the lenses of his glasses. "But?"

"But it seems to scare the hell out of anyone else who's read it," I finished.

One of the man's wiry salt-and-pepper eyebrows arched. "Is that so?"

"Yes. Why?"

He dropped his gaze back down to the dust jacket, which he had unfolded and spread out along the desktop. He smoothed out the creases with one gnarled, hairy-knuckled hand. His fingers traced the detail of the pencil-drawn artwork, caressed the blocky text of the title and my name.

"My cousin, Pembroke, would be the one to call about this," Finter said.

"Then let's call him."

"He's vanished."

"Vanished?"

"Disappeared. Gone." He waved a hand at the book. "These types of books can be...dangerous."

"All honest books are dangerous books," I said.

Finter looked up sharply. "What's that?"

"Just something I used to tell my students."

"This book here," he said, tapping not the book but the dust jacket. "This is not an honest book."

"No?"

"It's a guise. A ruse."

"What exactly does that mean?"

"It means that you've been baited by it, and now you're on the hook, my friend." The smile Ross Finter summoned to his lips possessed no humor, no good nature. It was like the smile the wolf gives Little Red Riding Hood. I felt a chill ripple up my spine. "It's the reason you find it boring while others, as you say, have had the hell scared out of them. It doesn't *want* them—in fact, it detracts them, makes them uncomfortable so they turn away from it and leave it alone. It's the poisonous frog with the brightly colored spots that say 'don't eat me or you'll die.'"

It was almost exactly what my agent had told me over the phone—that the book didn't *want* to be read. Not by her, anyway.

"But *you*," Finter continued. "You say it's boring, that nothing happens. You search through it, perhaps, trying to find the important things you may have missed. Correct?"

"Yes."

"But you still cannot find anything."

"That's right."

"Yet it holds your attention, keeps you captive. It's become something of an obsession, I'll even bet. Yes?"

"Yes. That's exactly right. How do you know that?"

"Baited," said Finter, not answering my question. "A guise."

"So if I'm *on* the hook, how do I get *off* it?" I asked.

"I'm not so sure that you do. However..." He curled a finger at me, then pointed down at the dust jacket. "Come. See here." He traced the blocky yellow text of my name. "The text was applied to the cover during the second part of a two-part offset printing process. Which means first you have the original artwork that is reproduced for the image on the cover, and then you have a secondary process—another layer, if you will— as the text for the title and author's name is applied."

"Okay," I said, not sure what was so significant about this revelation.

"There is artwork beneath the text," Finter went on. "See how the swirling clouds that make up the sky exist behind the lettering?"

"Yes."

"Well, there is more." He pressed an index finger over the first letter of my name—the W. "There is more than swirling sky behind your name. There is something else. See? See here? How brief little lines protrude from the corners, sticking out only slightly from behind your name. Do you see?"

I leaned over the desk and studied the dust jacket in the sunlight. "Yes," I said. "I see. There's something written in pencil behind the text of my name."

"Something that appears on the original artwork but has been covered up by the text," Finter said. "A word. Or possibly—"

"A name," I finished for him. "The artist's name?"

"It's anyone's guess. But if you find the original artwork, then you can see what your name covers up."

"And how the hell do I do that?"

"That," said Finter, "I cannot tell you."

I thanked him and left the bookstore, the copy of *Mr. Cables* back in its plastic bag and tucked under my arm. As I stepped out onto the sidewalk, the cold struck me, and I buttoned my coat.

A commuter bus lumbered slowly in front of the bookstore, a shiny metallic dinosaur that glinted with sunlight. I stared up at it as it passed, and at the slack profiles in the windows. I kept expecting to find one of the riders staring back at me—a figure in an outdated fedora whose brim cast his face in shadow.

I shivered just thinking about it.

The bus chugged toward the intersection, clouds of black exhaust belching from its tailpipe. When it stopped at the crosswalk, I felt my entire body go rigid. I was certain a man who fit the description of the swarthy, noirish Mr. Cables would step off. But the doors did not open, and a moment later, the commuter bus was groaning through the intersection and merging with traffic.

8

AN HOUR INTO MY drive back home, my cell phone chirped. I dug it out of my pocket.

"Wilson." It was my agent. "Those pages you sent me..."

"Yes?"

"Is it a joke?"

"What do you mean?"

"This isn't your work. Did you copy it straight from that book?"

"Susan, I don't know what you're talking about."

"Listen, if this is some kind of hoax, Wil, I don't know what the point is. I told you I didn't want to read anymore of that stuff."

"Susan, I don't know what the heck you're talking about. I sent you pages of the novel I've been working on."

"You can—Wilson—I can't even—"

Static was devouring the line.

"Susan, I can't hear you. Are you in Montauk? We must have a bad connection."

"...can't read anymore..."

"Susan? Susan?"

Static overrode the connection. Then there was nothing but silence.

I ended the call, remembering how Finter had picked up his receiver back at the shop and commented that the phone was working perfectly fine despite my inability to call his store. *This book here,* Finter had said. *This is not an honest book.*

"What are you, jamming the signal?" I said to the book, unsure what was crazier—that I was talking to a book or that I was beginning to believe it possessed the power to do exactly what I'd just accused it of.

When I was able, I pulled onto the shoulder of the road and pulled up my emails on my cell. In the SENT file, I found the email I'd sent off to Susan containing the chapters of my latest novel. I tapped the Word document icon and the attachment downloaded to my phone.

I stared at it, unsure of what I was looking at. But no—that wasn't the truth. I knew what it was. The pages were reproductions of text from *Mr. Cables*. Not photocopies, which I'd sent my agent previously, but hammered out in a Word document, presumably by me.

That couldn't be. There was some mistake. Some cosmic wires had gotten crossed. I'd sent Susan the wrong file, simple as that.

Then who typed up these pages? Who reproduced text from the novel onto this file? Who—

Then, all at once, it came to me...and with it, a cold tightening in my chest. *This isn't your work*, Susan had just said. *Did you copy it straight from that book?* And on the heels of that, I could picture Ross Finter studying me from over the rimless lenses of his glasses, scrutinizing me, asking if I knew which book was missing from my bio, and me responding that I did not, and Finter saying, *Are you sure?* As if I'd just told him a lie...

I glanced down at the passenger seat. The book had somehow gotten free of the plastic bag and was sitting on the seat upside-down, so that my outdated author photo stared up at me. I turned it over to reveal the sketch of Primrose Avenue on the front cover and that cold constriction in my chest grew tighter.

It was tied together too neatly, I suddenly realized, for it to be a mere confluence of circumstances, of coincidence layered upon coincidence. Primrose Avenue. Montclair Community College. A solitary book missing from my bio. No longer just mysterious and confounding, these things now conspired to point an accusatory finger at me that, until this very moment, I had missed. My God, I had *missed* it.

"Jesus Christ, it can't be..."

My heart jack-hammering in my chest, I fumbled the cell phone back into my pocket, then pulled back onto the highway. Instead of heading home, I took the first exit and rerouted toward a new destination.

It can't be possible...

I recalled the Montclair Community College's library boasting a vast collection of artwork on its walls, done by local artists, faculty members, and students. Many were simple pencil sketches, much like the artwork on the dust jacket of the book. And of course, if the artwork was truly a reproduction of Primrose Avenue—the street that bordered one side of the college campus—then it was possible the *original* piece was framed somewhere in that library. It was a stretch, but it was the only thing I could think of at that moment. And if the picture *was* there, and if it held the artist's name—*his* name—then...

Well, then I would know.

Impossible...

So was the book sitting on the passenger seat beside me.

I drove, and when the silence became too unnerving, I clicked on the radio and flooded the car with Christmas music.

9

NEARLY TWO DECADES HAD passed since I'd been to Montclair Community College. In those intervening years, I'd lost some hair, gained a few extra pounds, and achieved a level of success the twenty-something English and creative writing instructor I'd once been could only dream about. The school had undergone a revitalization, and boasted a collection of attractive glass buildings where there had previously only been squat brick boxcar-like structures, no doubt filled with asbestos and lead paint. For a moment I worried that the old library had been replaced, too, but as I drove alongside the campus just off the highway, I could see the old library and surrounding quad had remained unchanged.

I took the first turn, and found myself on Primrose Avenue. The houses here were unchanged as well, each little A-frame corralled behind whitewashed fences. The lampposts that lined the sidewalk were decorated with Christmas wreaths. Back when I'd taught here, I'd lived in one of these houses, rented it from someone in the English department. After all this time I'd forgotten the address, but as I coasted up the street, my gaze fell upon the house. It had been repainted a garish periwinkle, and its front porch was overflowing with half-dead plants spooling out of hanging baskets. The yard was overgrown, and there was a motorcycle parked in the driveway. For some reason the sight of that motorcycle bothered me, and would remain imprinted on my brain like the afterimage of a flashbulb.

I thought about stopping, about going up to the door and knocking, but decided not to. There was a small voice in the back of my head that told me I'd find nothing in that old place—nothing that would help with my current situation, anyway. What I was looking for—if it actually existed, of course—would be in the school's library.

At the end of the block, I pulled into one of the campus parking lots. What I originally thought was spume kicked up from puddles in the road was actually a gentle snowfall, and as I stepped out of the car, I could feel the cold droplets landing on my face and gathering in my eyelashes.

The campus was a ghost town. It occurred to me, as I campaigned across the quad to the library, that the students were probably on Christmas break. Would that mean the library would be closed until after the holidays?

"Can't catch a break," I muttered, moving swiftly through the cold toward the library doors, which looked all but shuttered against the fading daylight. When I felt something pressing against my ribs, I looked down to see that I was carrying the book. I'd taken it off the passenger seat without realizing it. It was as if the damn thing had become part of me.

I mounted the brick steps to the library doors, reached out for one of the long aluminum handles, and gave it a tug. To my surprise, the door swung open. A blast of heat greeted me, and I stepped hurriedly inside the building.

If Finter's Manhattan bookshop had been a submarine corridor, the Montclair Community College library was a vast mausoleum—equally as silent and unused, only much larger. My footfalls echoed along the tiled entranceway. On both sides of the foyer were glass cases filled with various trophies, ribbons, awards, photographs. The school's green-and-gold colors were everywhere, with a little red bunting added for the Christmas season.

The library was just as I remembered it. I had done hours of writing here in my twenties, between classes or in the evenings, and it was as if they hadn't even rearranged the tables. The librarian's desk—currently unoccupied—took up one whole wall. Beyond, I could see the study carrels and the stacks of nonfiction texts. The only change I could see was that the microfiche machines had been replaced with computer terminals. Also, the giant chest of drawers that had housed the Dewey decimal cards had been replaced by a display of hardcover books; there was a sign posted on the table that read NOTABLE READS, and as I walked by it, I saw a few of my novels among the titles.

I froze in mid-step and stared at the table of my books—at one book in particular. My first published novel. A hardcover edition, wrapped in Mylar and standing at the top of a pyramid of my other books.

"Hey, man," said a voice. I spun around to see a slender fellow in a checked flannel shirt rummaging among a stack of books on a cart. He was maybe in his early twenties, possibly a student aide. "Did you need help with anything?"

"There used to be artwork on the walls. Drawings and paintings done by the faculty and students."

"There's some framed pictures in the back, by the poetry stacks."

"Thanks."

"Anything in particular you're looking for?"

I nearly held up *Mr. Cables* and showed him the artwork on the cover, but caught myself at the last minute. As it was, the guy was staring at the book cradled against my side, as if I'd shoplifted it.

"Not really. I used to teach here."

"Yeah? Well, let me know if I can do anything for you."

"Will do. Thanks."

I walked down the center of the library toward the poetry section. I could *smell* the books—that musty parchment odor that was as comforting as a warm bed. Yet despite the comfort of that smell, a tremor of apprehension was coursing through me. It had hit me like a slap in the car, had been gaining strength on the drive to Montclair, and had only increased as I got out of the car and crossed the parking lot to the quad. Now, it rattled me to the point that my teeth began to chatter. I tried to convince myself that my supposition was wrong, that this was all going to prove to be an inexplicable series of coincidences, that what I *feared* could not actually *be*.

Are you sure? Ross Finter whispered in my head.

I crossed between two shelves labeled POETRY and saw that the walls back here were adorned with framed artwork—watercolor paintings, charcoal sketches, collages made from magazine clippings. There were sculptures here, too—modern-art pieces comprised of metal rings and sprockets, household items, papier-mâché masks on wooden pedestals.

I walked the length of the wall, studying the framed artwork. With each passing minute, I grew slightly more hopeful that I had been wrong and that the secret to *Mr. Cables* had nothing to do with what had happened all those years ago at this school, had nothing to do with *him*. In fact, I was just about to give up the search when I noticed a stack of framed pictures leaning against a wall, partially hidden behind a photocopier. Either these hadn't been hung up yet, or they had recently been taken down—either way, I went to them, dropped to my knees, and rifled through them. Sweat tickled the side of my face despite the chill I felt at the center of my bones.

And then there it was—the pencil-sketch of Primrose Avenue that was the source of the artwork reproduced on the book's dust jacket.

"No," I mumbled.

Yet I couldn't help myself. I slid the frame out from the stack and held it up to my face. Swiping a film of dust off the glass, there was no denying that it was the same picture. It was about twice the size of the image on the dust jacket, but that didn't make it any easier to make out the details in the hazy swirls and crosshatches of pencilwork.

There was no word or name drawn in the sky above the houses, as there appeared to be beneath my name on the book's dust jacket. This was because the dimensions were off—the dust jacket was taller, while the actual drawing was longer and narrower. If there had ever been a name written in the sky of the original, it had been cut away to fit the frame.

Are you sure? whispered Finter.

Then I saw something at the bottom right-hand corner of the drawing—what appeared to be the artist's signature scrawled in pencil. I could make out the tops of the letters, but the bulk of the name was covered by the frame.

I cast a glance over my shoulder, then turned the frame over in my lap. I pried back the staples that held the cardboard backing in place, then stripped the drawing out of the frame altogether.

The name of the artist was Tony Meeks.

I felt my stomach drop at the sight of it.

Of course it's Tony, said a small voice in the back of my head. I leaned back against a bookshelf before I passed out. *Of course it is. It all makes sense now, doesn't it? You've solved the mystery of this haunting, Professor. And you may have done so sooner if you weren't so arrogant, if you'd ever felt a single ounce of remorse. So here we are, Professor. You were right.*

Yes.

I was right.

10

IN 1999, I ACHIEVED a certain morbid celebrity after a student of mine, Tony Meeks, was killed in a motorcycle accident. He had been a quiet, abashed sort of fellow who was somehow always more noticeable in periphery than he was if you looked straight at him. He was tall, with an undisciplined mop of black hair, and sharp, wolfish eyes that always seemed to peer out at you from beneath a slightly downturned brow. Despite his tallness, his face was an assemblage of delicate, almost effeminate features, and he possessed the neatly manicured and articulate hands of a surgeon. His clothes always looked second-rate, an ensemble of faded dungarees, motorcycle boots, flannel shirts, and a military-style surplus jacket with ambiguous insignias on the sleeves. Whenever he shifted in his seat, I could hear the chain clipped to his wallet clang against the chair leg.

I had him for just one class, Creative Writing 101, where he would sit in the back of the room, nearly with his back against the wall, as though it were his intention to become part of the masonry. On the rare occasions when he spoke, be it aloud to the rest of the class when answering a question or in a more intimate one-on-one setting in my office, he gave the impression that he was doing so with reluctance, even if he was the one to have initiated the dialogue. There was the slightest backwoods drawl to his speech, though you really had to listen for it, and I remember thinking that maybe he didn't talk so much because he was embarrassed by it.

I don't believe he had many friends at the college. It wasn't that the other students disliked him. No one knew him well enough to dislike him. The few times I'd glimpsed him, shuffling with his head down across the quad or curled vulture-like over a Styrofoam bowl of vegetable stew in the cafeteria, he was always alone. Sometimes I would see him sitting on a bench by himself along the path that wound between Pratt Hall and the modular little annex that looked like a trailer, his face buried in a paperback novel or in one of his notebooks as he scribbled wildly, that dark hair hanging down over his eyes in unruly curlicues.

Halfway through the semester, I paired students up to collaborate on a short piece of fiction. I joined Tony Meeks up with a similarly introverted student, Eric Mayfield, because I incorrectly assumed they might find some commonality in their brooding. However, when Mayfield handed in the assignment, I could tell from the disjointed tone of the writing as well as the dejected look on Mayfield's face that my supposition had been incorrect. There hadn't been any collaboration between the two, and my guess was that Meeks had simply typed up some random passages which he then provided to Mayfield, who included them in the body of his own half-finished story, desperate to make some vague sense of it all.

Meeks was just six days shy of his twentieth birthday when the tires of his 1972 Yamaha motorcycle surrendered their grip on the asphalt of Primrose Avenue, firing the bike up and over a guardrail while simultaneously propelling Meeks into the air. Police recovered his body over two hundred and fifty feet from the site of the crash, his motorcycle boots stripped from his feet and his surplus jacket shredded to bloody ribbons. He must have been going pretty fast, and he hadn't been wearing a helmet. According to the toxicology report, there were no traces of alcohol or narcotics in his system. Perhaps he had simply been speeding and lost control of the bike.

I read about the accident in the newspaper. Other things I happened to overhear on campus—in the hallways, restrooms, even the teachers' lounge. Some even suggested that maybe the crash hadn't been an accident at all. He was a loner, a solitary shadow creeping among the redbrick hallways and puke-green linoleum of Montclair Community College. If ever there had been a man bent on vehicular suicide, it was the inauspicious artist and wannabe writer in the military surplus jacket.

I hadn't known Tony Meeks well enough to formulate my own opinion about his death, be it accident or deliberate. I had hardly known him at all, really. Comments about him being nothing more than a shadow were pretty accurate. He had been a talented writer and artist—a few of his sketches had been put on display in the college library and behind a display case in the humanities building—but he was shy, reserved, distant. Yet despite how unassuming and practically invisible he had been when he was alive, I came to find Tony Meeks's empty desk at the back of my classroom somewhat troubling in its conspicuousness in the days and weeks following his death. I began to suffer dreams in which I came to understand that the empty desk was in fact not empty at all; I could feel Meeks's eyes on me, watching me from the back of that room, even though I couldn't see him. I would turn to write something on the chalkboard, and that was when I'd hear the familiar clink of his wallet chain against the hollow metal chair leg. Or I would be out in the quad, the sun blazing through a bank of pinkish spring clouds, when I'd glimpse his murky slump-shouldered form vanishing between two buildings. These nightmares plagued me.

Two weeks before his death, I asked Tony to stay after class. Reluctantly, he'd remained seated at his desk at the back of the room after all the other students had filtered out into the hallway. Fairly certain he wasn't going to come up to my desk, I approached him, opting to sit on the edge of the desk in front of him.

"Why are you taking this class?" I asked him.

His smooth, effeminate features seemed to slacken. Yet his eyes remained dark and fixed on me. "What do you mean?" he said, his voice just above a whisper. He feigned interest in digging something out of the sole of his motorcycle boot.

"I mean you're so much better than the rest of these guys. Creative Writing 101 is a throwaway elective. You should be in an advanced class."

"I like this class."

"Yeah, but are you getting anything out of it?"

He seemed to consider this, dropping his eyes to whatever he was digging at in his boot, black commas of hair curtaining his forehead.

"Have you ever submitted any of your stories for publication?" I asked him.

"Are you kidding?"

"No," I said. "I'm not."

"I wouldn't know where to start."

"Well, there's the campus literary magazine, for one. Not the most highbrow lit journal on the planet, I agree, but it might give you some sense of accomplishment."

To my surprise, he laughed. It was a sharp whip-crack, and it startled me. "Do they pay anything?" he asked.

"No, they don't. No money, anyway. Just contributor copies."

"It doesn't matter. I write for myself."

"That's why you're so good."

Those dark eyes found me again, but they didn't linger this time. Just as quickly as he had looked up at me, he turned his attention toward the wall of windows that looked out on the quad. Outside, some students stood smoking cigarettes by one of the campus security boxes—a phone-booth-shaped callbox with a blue light on top, which all the students referred to as rape boxes.

"Listen," I said. "Have you written anything longer than short stories? Maybe a novelette or something?"

"Oh," he said, looking back down at his motorcycle boot. There was a gritty piece of chewing gum stuck to the heel, which he dug at with his neatly-trimmed fingernails. "I've written a novel."

"Have you? What's it called?"

"I don't know. I don't have a title yet."

"What's it about?"

"Just...I don't know. Stuff."

"Would you mind if I read it? Maybe I could give you some pointers, point you in the right direction."

Again, Tony Meeks's girlish features seemed to smooth out so that there was hardly a crease in his face. Even the lines that bracketed his mouth vanished into that seamless valley. He looked like an infant expelled from the womb. "You know about that kind of thing? Publishing novels and whatever?"

What I knew was that I'd written my fair share of novel manuscripts, none of which amounted to the proverbial hill of beans. I'd submitted a few to agents and small presses, but no one had been interested in representing or publishing me. But I could certainly read this kid's work and offer him some advice about plot, structure, character, whatever it might lack. I told him as much, and he seemed surprised.

"You'd do that for me?" he said.

"Sure. Heck, if it's good enough, maybe we can find you an agent."

He laughed—this time there was more musicality to the sound—and when I smiled in return, he seemed to relax for the first time since I'd come over and sat on the edge of the desk.

"Thanks, Mr. Paventeau. I'll bring it in next week."

"Looking forward to it."

"And if it stinks, just say the word."

"I'll be honest, I promise," I told him. "But I don't think it'll stink."

"Righteous," he said, nodding his head. When he reached down for the straps of his backpack, I knew he was ready to leave.

"Just do me one favor, will you?" I said.

"What's that?"

"This is a creative writing class. There aren't any exams, any tests. Your final grade is split between the grades you get on your written assignments and your class participation. Which, as you know, is practically nil."

"I don't like speaking in public."

"It's thirteen students."

"I don't like speaking in front of thirteen students," he retorted, and I could sense a vein of effrontery in his tone now.

"Well, let's see if we can work on that, all right?"

"Yeah, all right, Mr. Paventeau."

"Have a good weekend, Tony," I told him, getting up off the desk and moving back toward the front of the room. I expected him to say something similar to me, but when I turned back around, I found he had slipped silently out the back door of the classroom.

True to his word, Tony Meeks came to class that Monday with a large white cake box tucked under one arm. Without uttering a sound, he set the box on the corner of my desk at the beginning of class, then skulked down the aisle to his seat. Truth be told, I gave the boxed manuscript very little thought, and stowed it away in my desk.

Later that week, with the spring wildflowers in full bloom in the courtyard and fat, lazy clouds scudding across a brilliant blue sky, I beckoned Tony Meeks to stand up and read one of his assignments aloud to the class.

"I'd rather not," he said.

His comment surprised me. A few of the other students looked around. As is typical of a creative writing class, there was never a shortage of people willing to read their sparkling, brilliant words to their peers—after all, everyone always applauded—so about a half dozen hands went up following Meeks's retort.

I smiled humorlessly, then told the other students to drop their hands. "Come on, Tony. It's a wonderful example of what this assignment is all about. I'd really like you to share it with the class."

"And I'd really rather not," he said.

I could have let it go at that, but I didn't. "Stand up, Tony," I called to him.

At first, Tony Meeks did not move. I watched the chain from his wallet swing hypnotically as he shifted with evident discomfort in his seat. He was gazing out from behind the filigreed curls of his hair, his head turned slightly downward so that his forehead looked more prominent than usual. Already I was wondering how far to push this; it wasn't as if I could force him to stand and read, and his continued refusal would only make me look powerless. But then, to my relief, he unfolded himself out from behind his desk and stood to his full height.

"Please," I said to him, going around my desk and settling down in the creaky wooden chair. "Go on and read."

His eyes never left mine. Even when he picked up the pages of his assignment and began to recite, his eyes remained fixed on me. At first I thought I saw disdain in his stare...but when I realized it was nothing more than a childlike embarrassment, I wished I hadn't pursued this with him and that I had let the whole thing go.

The assignment was for the students to write their own obituaries. It was a fun exercise that usually elicited some laughs, and there were usually two or three students who learned something about themselves in the process. Most students saw themselves living lives of grandeur, pomposity, dreams that in real life would most likely never reach fulfillment. That was part of the fun of the assignment, after all—to look back on a crazy life that was never lived. But Tony Meeks's obituary had been humble and eerily realistic. He had even misspelled his last name, *Meaks*, showing that who he was and what he may or may not have accomplished prior to his death meant very little to whoever might write about it. It was sadly unpretentious and extremely well-written.

So Tony Meeks read his obituary aloud. It was beautiful in its simplicity, and despite his reticence to read it to his peers, he received an ovation after he was done.

And the whole time, his eyes never left mine.

Once the class cleared out, it was my intention to speak one-on-one with him, as he was generally a slow mover and one of the last students to shuffle out of the classroom. I had wanted to beam pride at him and thank him for reading aloud, and wasn't it a wonderful thing? Didn't he feel good getting those words out of him and sharing them with the rest of the class? But he was quick that day—out the door like a jackrabbit.

The following afternoon, I read about his death in the newspaper.

My aforementioned celebrity came in the form of rumors that began circulating throughout the college immediately after Tony Meeks's death. Some of my more superstitious students had begun to apply some correlation between Tony Meeks's death and my insistence that he stand before the classroom and read his obituary just hours before the fatal motorcycle accident. I was informed by some of my colleagues that some students referred to me as Professor Death. I laughed it off, suggesting that the name had a nice Marvel Comics ring to it. But in truth, the kid's death troubled me.

I waited a full month after the accident before I read Tony's novel. One evening, I poured myself a glass of Dewar's, as if to drink to poor Tony's memory, then settled in the living room of the rented house on Primrose Avenue with the cake box in my lap.

He had told me his novel had no title. But when I opened the lid of the box, I saw that he had typed THE BODY FIELDS in all caps in the center of the page. Below that—A NOVEL OF SUSPENSE BY ANTHONY MEEKS. Unlike the assignments he had turned in for class, which had been written on a PC or laptop and printed on a standard laser printer, it seemed the manuscript had been typed on an old manual typewriter.

I read the whole manuscript in two days. It was brilliant. The assuredness of the voice, the economy of word, the perfect plot structure—it was like a goddamn primer on how to write a suspense novel.

Yet instead of inspiring me, it sent me spiraling into a dark depression. I began to drink more than usual, and my demeanor around the campus became one of curtness and agitation. I was like someone itching for a fight. Nights, I lay awake listening to the sounds of the traffic on Primrose. I attempted to resurrect some older novel manuscripts I'd kept from years earlier, but these were petrified dead things, incapable of revivification. I was dating a woman around this time, but she ultimately left me because of my depressive mood. I could hardly blame her.

Excuses could be made, though in truth, I don't remember thinking things out too well. I guess maybe I made the mistake of looking at the tips of my fingers too closely one afternoon, examining those whorls and valleys and tributaries that conspire to lend me identity, and I realized that people—all people—were just random assorted pieces indiscriminately compiled to suggested who they are as a whole. I put those fingertips to work, and spent just over a week retyping Tony Meeks's manuscript. I tightened up the narrative and changed some names, but in the end, I altered very little and even kept the title. When I was done, I typed my name below the title, then sent the manuscript to a literary agent whom I'd met at a writing seminar a few years earlier. Two weeks later I signed with that agent, and a few months after that, this agent sold the manuscript to a major New York house. The book hit the *New York Times* bestseller list, and Wilson S. Paventeau's life had changed forever.

11

IT WAS LATE BY the time I returned home from Montclair. The house was dark, and I hurried from the car to the front porch as if someone—or something—was chasing me. Inside, I turned on all the downstairs lights before removing my coat. When I realized I was still clutching the copy of *Mr. Cables*, I chucked it across the living room. It fell behind the sofa, and I could hear the dust jacket tearing as it struck the floor.

Not good enough, I thought, shoving the sofa aside and snatching the book up off the floor. I went to the fireplace, kicked aside the metal grate, and tossed the book into the hearth. There was a lighter in a junk drawer, which I grabbed up and brought over to the fireplace. Kneeling down, I flicked the lighter and touched the tongue of flame to the corner of the book. It didn't catch at first...but then a small blue runner of fire lifted off the book cover and rose to a bright orange flame.

Will that really change anything? said the voice in my head.

For a second, I thought someone was watching me from beyond the wall of windows. But that was impossible, because the rear of the house was built on a bluff that overlooked the forest. The rear of the house was two stories aboveground.

This changes nothing, said the voice.

"Goddamn it," I growled, then blew the flame out. I dug the book out of the fireplace and patted the charred corner with my hand. Black ash drifted to the floor.

The voice was right; destroying the book was no solution.

I sat down hard and leaned against the sofa. My heart felt like a punching bag in my chest. For a long time, I stared at the copy of *Mr. Cables* on the floor at my feet. I was thinking of it as a *copy* of a book, when in reality it was the only one. The original. It was Mr. Cables himself.

I dragged myself to my feet and went down into the basement. In a backroom, I shoved some old clothes and holiday decorations out of the way, revealing an old steamer trunk tucked up against the wall. It contained all of the original versions of my early manuscripts, back when I used to edit off the printed page. I opened the trunk and dug through the cake boxes inside, the stacks of printed pages held together by rubber bands, and the yellow legal pads riddled with notes. At the bottom of the trunk was Tony Meeks's original cake box, which contained the typewritten version of his manuscript. I opened the box and saw Tony's manuscript inside. I took the manuscript from the box, feeling its weight in my hands, and thumbed through it. I had corrupted it by making notes in the margin. I had crossed out a word here and there, changed a few character names. I realized that, based on my editor's suggestion, I had removed a block of exposition that hadn't advanced the story, starting with page thirty-three. I flipped through the pages and saw that they corresponded with the pages that were missing from *Mr. Cables*.

I felt like I was losing my mind.

The last page of the manuscript contained Tony Meeks's contact information, including his home address, where he'd lived with his parents and siblings while attending Montclair Community College.

A small town called Quimby.

12

I SET OUT EARLY the next morning, just as the first real snowfall of the season descended upon my small place in the world. My neighbor's chimney was at it again, unfurling a pennant of grayish smoke into the atmosphere.

I had no idea if Tony Meeks's family still lived at the Quimby address, but I figured that, given the series of discoveries that had led me here, there was a good chance they still did. Beside me on the passenger seat was *Mr. Cables*, with its torn dust jacket and charred corner. My terrible copilot.

The snowfall had turned into a blizzard by the time I reached Quimby. The town was really just a main road flanked on either side by decrepit single-family homes, a blue-collar New Jersey neighborhood that had continued to deteriorate as local factories closed or moved elsewhere. It was Norman Rockwell after the Apocalypse. I drove slowly down the street, peering at the numbers on the houses until I located the right address.

The house had a section of tarp on the roof and was missing some siding. There were two pickup trucks in the driveway collecting snow, and some plastic riding toys strewn about the porch. There was a detached garage out back, its doors open, and I could see a few motorcycles and an ATV inside. Their mailbox was fashioned to look like a mallard, its wooden propeller-wings spinning in the wind.

I parked along the curb and got out. The temperature had dropped about fifteen degrees, and I was feeling it in my marrow now.

Meteorologists were forecasting a long winter and I found that, for the first time in forever, the thought of being snowed in at my house terrified me.

It wasn't until I'd already knocked on the front door that I realized I was holding *Mr. Cables* in both hands, as if to present it as a gift to whoever answered the door. I quickly dropped my hands and tucked the book under one arm.

The door opened and a young girl, perhaps five or six years old, peered up at me.

"Uh, hi," I said. "Is your mom or dad at home?"

The little girl shook her head.

"How about a grownup?"

The little girl withdrew into the house and shouted for someone named Nanoo. I stood there, shifting my weight from one foot to the other, sweating in my coat despite the cold that funneled through me. The propeller-wings of the mallard mailbox squealed as they spun.

A woman appeared in the doorway. She was maybe in her early seventies, with silver-streaked hair pulled back into a bun. Her face was as weathered and seamed as an old catcher's mitt, but her eyes were kind.

"Hello," I said. "I'm looking for Mr. and Mrs. Meeks."

"I'm Gloria Meeks," said the woman.

"My name is Wilson Paventeau. I used to teach at the community college in Montclair. Tony Meeks was a student of mine."

"Oh." The kindness in the woman's eyes dulled. There was a fragility about her that was disconcerting, as if a strong wind might reduce her to a pile of gray powder. "Yes. I'm Tony's mother. Won't you come in?"

"Thank you."

She stepped aside, and I entered a foyer that was wallpapered in a busy floral design. I could smell something cooking in the kitchen, and the heat pumping from the baseboards nearly bowled me over. I suddenly felt clammy and sick.

"Was there something we can do for you?" she asked.

"Well, I wanted to talk to you and your husband, if he's...if he's around...and it may take some time. It's about Tony."

"Tony?"

"I know this is coming out of the blue, ma'am. But I'd really appreciate your time."

"All right." She touched the young girl on her shoulder and said, "Baby, go to the back door and tell Goompa to come inside, will you?"

The girl nodded, and was already streaming down the hallway before the woman turned back to me.

"Can I get you a drink or something, Mr. Paventeau?"

"Water would be great, thanks."

"Have a seat inside," she said, motioning toward a stuffy little living room. There was a loveseat and a Christmas tree and a fireplace with stockings hanging from the mantel and dog hair all over everything.

"Thank you," I said, and sat in the loveseat. From here, I could see out the windows toward the back of the house. An older gentleman in a checked hunting jacket and ski cap came out of the garage. He kicked the snow off his boots as he climbed the rear steps of the house.

I realized the book was in my lap now. I set it on the cushion beside me, not wanting it to touch me. I felt like a traitor in this house.

That's because you are, said the voice in my head.

"Cut it out," I muttered.

Something whined. I looked and saw a Golden Retriever watching me from the hallway. Despite the Christmas bells that hung from its collar, it had sneaked up on me.

"Mr. Paventeau, is it?" said the man in the hunting jacket as he came into the room. He was a large man whose presence alone was enough to fill the living room. He possessed the broad forehead and dark, contemplative eyes I remembered his son having.

I stood, but he motioned for me to sit back down. I shook his hand from a crouched position, and he introduced himself as Arnold Meeks. He sat opposite me in an armchair, crossing his legs. He'd removed his boots, and I could see the holes at the bottom of one sock.

Gloria entered and handed me a glass of water. I drank half of it, then cradled the glass in my lap. Gloria sat on an ottoman beside her husband's armchair.

"I taught your son back in 1999," I said. "At Montclair Community. He was a talented kid. Probably the most talented student I ever had. I'm so sorry for your loss."

"Thank you," said the man. He reached over and gathered up his wife's hand, squeezed it.

"Listen, I don't know how to say this, so I'm just going to come out with it," I said, and told them about how their son had given me a novel manuscript just before he died, and how I'd subsequently published it as my own. Their expressions did not change throughout my telling, and when I finished, the room sank into silence. The Golden Retriever watching from the hallway held more expression on its face than Tony Meeks's parents.

"Here," I said, digging a paperback copy of *The Body Fields* from my coat pocket. I handed it to Arnold, who clutched it in two big hands while his wife peered at it from over his shoulder.

Finally, Gloria Meeks said, "Well, that's nice, isn't it?"

"Is it?" I said.

"So this book," Arnold interjected, handing the paperback to his wife. "It came out in bookstores and everything?"

"Yes. It's still in print."

"And you can just...go in a store and buy it?"

"Yes," I said.

"Well." And a broad smile carved its way across Arnold Meeks's face. He turned to his wife. "Look at that, will ya?"

"Anthony had always wanted to be a writer," Gloria said. She caressed the paperback's glossy cover. It was one of my more subtle covers, depicting the silhouette of a farmhouse in a field at dusk. I was suddenly grateful for the subtlety of it. "Since he was a little boy. He used to write all these little stories in these memo books—"

"Drew pictures, too," said Arnold. "He was a wonderful artist."

"I remember we used to take the bus into the city once a month," Gloria went on, "and he'd sit there with this memo pad and just make little notes, write down little observations, about all the people he'd see on the bus. He'd make up stories about them, and I was always amazed at the strength of his imagination. Isn't that something? Oh, he couldn't have been more than eight years old."

"He was a talented kid," Arnold said. "I got a bike out back, he did all the airbrushing himself. You should see it. It's a beaut."

"I don't think you folks understood what I said," I told them. "About the book. About what I did."

"You got our boy's book published," said Arnold.

"Yes, but it was under my name. I put my name on it."

"But these are his words, right?" Gloria said, and she clutched the paperback to her chest as if it were something valuable that she'd long since misplaced. "This is Anthony's story, isn't it?"

"Yes, but—"

"And here it is," said Arnold, "for all the world to see. I think that's really something."

"It really is," said Gloria.

"No," I said. "No, it's got my name on it. I published it as my own."

"I heard that all those celebrities hire people to write their books," said Gloria. "Is that true?"

"This is different. I stole the book from your son."

"Oh, now," Arnold said, waving a hand at me. "The important thing is it's out there, right? People can read our boy's story. That's the important thing, isn't it?" When I didn't respond, he repeated the question: "Isn't it?"

"I don't know," I said. It was true—I had no idea anymore. I'd lost myself somewhere along the way and didn't know right from wrong, good from bad, an honest book from a dishonest book.

"Until you showed up, Mr. Paventeau, we never knew this book existed. We never knew there was more of our boy out there in the world. And now we've got his words, don't we?"

"We've got another piece of him," added Gloria. "So thank you. Thank you."

I cleared my throat, found my voice, and said, "There's also a sizable amount of money."

"How's that?" Arnold and Gloria said at the same time.

"Your son's book was a bestseller. It's earned quite a bit of money over the years. It was optioned for a movie twice."

"A movie?" Gloria said, her eyes going wide.

"It's a lot of money," I said, digging a cashier's check out of my coat pocket. "Your son earned it. It should go to you."

"Oh, listen, we don't need for nothing," Gloria said as I handed the check to her husband. "We're really getting along just—"

"Jesus, boy," Arnold said, looking at the check. "This can't be real." He looked up at me. "Is this some kind of come-on?"

"No, sir."

Gloria took the check from him. Her eyes lit up. "Dear God," she uttered.

"There's more," I told them. "I'll have my agent send you the royalties from here on out, too."

"We can't take this, Mr. Paventeau," Gloria said, holding the check out to me. I saw her husband's eyes shift in her direction, a clear signal that he perhaps didn't share his wife's sentiment.

"What about that little girl?" I asked. "Is she your granddaughter?"

"One of nine!" Gloria said proudly. "We've got nine grandchildren, Mr. Paventeau. Anthony had three siblings, did you know that? And they each have three kids of their own."

I'd read something about siblings in Tony's obituary—his *real* obituary—all those years ago, but I couldn't remember the details.

"Listen," I said. "I probably wouldn't have a writing career if it wasn't for that first book—your son's book—so maybe I owe you everything I have. I don't know. I'm...I'm confused..."

"Son," Arnold said, leaning closer to me from his armchair. "There's no need to be confused, okay? There's no need to be confused."

"Okay," I said, nodding. "Okay. But please take the money. Give it to your grandkids. It's Tony's money, and it should stay in your family."

"All right, son," said Arnold. He took the check from his wife and made it disappear inside the breast pocket of his chambray shirt.

Gloria stood. She touched her husband on the shoulder but her eyes remained on me. "It was so good of you to come out this way, especially in this weather, Mr. Paventeau."

"I'm not sure I had a choice," I said.

"Will you stay for supper?"

"Oh, no. I really can't."

"Look at all that snow," Gloria said, migrating toward the front windows. It was really coming down now.

"I'll be okay," I assured her. I set the water glass on an end table, gathered *Mr. Cables* from the loveseat, and stood. "I should probably get back on the road."

"You've gotta come see the airbrush work Anthony did on the bike first," Arnold said. He grunted as he hoisted himself out of the armchair.

"All right," I said. Then something occurred to me. "Have either of you ever heard of anyone called Mr. Cables?"

A look of utter stupefaction fell upon both their faces. They exchanged a glance, and for the first time since my arrival, Arnold Meeks's gaze turned suspicious. "Mr. Cables," he said. "How'd you..."

"How do you know about Mr. Cables?" Gloria said.

Because I didn't want these people to think I was crazy, I said, "Tony wrote about him in class. In one of his stories."

"Mr. Cables was Tony's nickname when he was younger," Gloria said. "I haven't heard that name in...oh, Lord, in such a long time. Isn't that right, Arnold? Lordy, I'd nearly forgotten."

Arnold put an arm around his wife's shoulders. She still held the paperback copy of *The Body Fields* to her breast.

"A nickname," I said. I glanced down at the book in my own hands.

"I'd all but forgotten," Gloria said. Her eyes were glassy now, threatening tears. She tented her hands beneath her nose, as if in prayer.

"When he was just a kid, he was hit by a car," Arnold said. "He spent weeks in traction, his leg all busted up and in a cast. They had him in the hospital room with his leg suspended by these cables to keep the swelling down. He was so scared. We called him Mr. Cables, and he liked that. The name stuck for—"

"For years," Gloria cut in. Her eyes were distant now, lost in a memory. "We called him that for years."

"Until he grew up," Arnold said. "Then there was no more Mr. Cables."

"I'm not so sure about that," I told them, but they weren't listening to me now. They were lost in reverie, somewhere with their dead son.

13

BEFORE LEAVING, I WENT out to the garage with Arnold Meeks, who showed me the airbrush work his son had done on an old Harley. It was a beautiful piece of artwork, reminiscent of van Gogh's *Starry Night*, a mosaic of color and textured swirls that seemed to hold hidden meaning the longer you stared at it. In that moment, I felt a bit of Tony Meeks right there with me, as he had been nearly two decades earlier in my creative writing class.

"It's wonderful," I said.

Arnold stood there beside me, staring at the bike. "I understood what you were telling my wife and me in there, Mr. Paventeau," he said, not looking at me. "What you did with our son's book, I mean. I'm not some naïve old fool."

I looked at him, stared at his profile as he studied his son's bike. The corner of his mouth twitched, and there was moisture collecting in his red-rimmed old eyes. He said no more about it, but his intention was suddenly clear. He was being kind enough to grant me absolution.

"Thank you," I told him.

"All right, then," Arnold Meeks said, swiping a hand across his eyes.

Behind the motorcycle, stacked against the wall of the garage, were several canvas paintings, the style of which was undeniably similar to the artwork on the bike. I pointed to them. "Were those Tony's?"

"Oh, sure. A writer and an artist, my boy. Wanna see some?"

"I'd like that."

Arnold squeezed behind the bike and began handing me one painting after another. I admired each abstract fusion of color, of shapes, of stark and heavy lines juxtaposed by soft brushstrokes. I was smiling to myself—something I only realized I was doing the moment it fled from my face.

On the canvas before me, a figure stood among the celestial swirls of color—a figure in a trench coat and fedora. The figure's face was a dark, smudgy shadow. I looked up at the remaining paintings against the wall and saw that this same figure—Mr. Cables—was on all of them. Sometimes he was obscured behind a pattern of dark brushstrokes; other times he was a figure in a crowd. One painting was a reproduction of the sketch that was back at the community college library, a version of which adorned the dust jacket of the hardback novel I now clutched to my hip.

Arnold registered my discomfort. He glanced down at the remaining paintings against the garage wall. "That's Mr. Cables right there," he said.

"I thought that was just a nickname."

Arnold straightened his back, and I heard the tendons pop. He came back around from behind the bike, rubbing at the back of his neck with a large hand. "That accident he was in when he was just a boy?"

"Hit by a car," I said. "Weeks in traction."

Arnold nodded. "Two days in a coma, too. He was still in the hospital when he started writing and drawing. It's like he came out of that coma with all the inspiration in the world. He was laid up for weeks with the leg, so there was nothing much else for him to do, but Lord, that boy went through some notebooks in that time. Always writing, always sketching little pictures." He mimed scribbling in the air. "The bug never left him. He was always so driven when it came to his art. Driven nearly into a frenzy, sometimes. He'd forget to eat, forget to sleep. Like the whole world would march on while he remained in his own little bubble, creating his art. I once asked him how he could *think* so much to write all those stories, and he said it wasn't him at all. Said it was Mr. Cables."

"Mr. Cables," I heard myself echo. I couldn't peel my gaze from the paintings of that fedora-clad wraith.

"Said Mr. Cables was his inspiration, his source of creativity. You writers got a word for it..."

"The muse," I said.

"Yeah, right. That's it. Mr. Cables went from being a nickname to being Tony's muse. Ain't that somethin'?"

I was incapable of speaking; I simply stared at those paintings.

"You gonna be okay, Mr. Paventeau?"

I looked up at him. "I don't know," I told him. "I'm sorry, you know. For what happened."

"It was an accident," he said.

"I'm sorry for what I did. I wanted to be a writer so badly I guess I'd do anything."

He smiled at me. "All honest writers are dangerous writers," he said.

His words jarred me.

"Just something Anthony had once said to me. It was right before he died. I asked him where he'd heard that and he said he just made it up."

I laughed. I couldn't help it. The whole thing was bizarre. Once I regained some measure of composure, I said, "He got that from me. I said that in class. He...he stole my words."

"Well," Arnold Meeks said, and he clapped me on the back. "There you go, then."

Yes.

There I go.

14

IT BECAME CLEAR TO me, standing there in the Meeks's garage, that I had fallen victim to possession. Not of the demonic variety, but of the artistic. The creative. My own muse—that insecure, over-thinking, overreaching, overwrought little fellow on whose shoulders I had constructed and maintained a successful career—had been usurped by one with hot claws and sharp fangs. One that was fierce and hungry and much stronger than my own. This wasn't an accident, but the result of my own actions. I had stolen the boy's words and thus inadvertently invited his muse to take up residence inside me.

It was all so ridiculous, I kept bursting into fits of laughter on the drive home. Terrible, illogical laughter. It caused my chest to ache and my eyes to periodically well up. At one point, as I motored along the turnpike, I happened to glance out the side window at a grungy-looking Greyhound bus lumbering in the lane beside me. I looked up at the bus's windows. They were all empty except for one, very close to the back. A figure sat there, staring out at me beneath a wide-brimmed fedora. His face was nothing but shadow, though two dim lights burned where his eyes should have been.

15

BEFORE RETURNING HOME, I stopped at the local grocery store and purchased every notebook they had in stock—the memo pads, the spiral-bound composition books, the yellow legal pads—as well as several packages of BIC Velocity pens. The tools for serious writing.

It was dusk by the time I pulled up the forested driveway toward my home, and the sky toward the east had already deepened to a spectral indigo, not unlike one of Tony Meeks's paintings. It wasn't too dark for me to miss the fresh footprints in the snow—the prints that circumnavigated my house. Prints that seemed to stop just outside my den window.

I would attempt to exorcise Mr. Cables from my creative consciousness the only way I knew how.

I would write him out.

16

THERE IS A PLACE you go to when you write. It can be as quaint as a European village or as vast as a collection of galaxies. You lift the sheet that is the fabric of the real world and slip beneath it to that place. Time stops, even if the little brass clock on the mantelpiece continues to tick, tick, tick.

In my den, I closed the glowing hatch of my laptop and removed it from my desk. I stacked the notebooks I had purchased—all of them—in neat piles. I opened the fresh packet of Velocity pens. I brewed a fresh pot of coffee but didn't drink too much of it, not wanting to interrupt my progress with frequent trips to the bathroom.

Seated at the desk, pen in hand, a blank memo pad opened before me, I wrote the first line:

The curious thing about Quimby was that he wasn't curious at all.

It was automatic. Sometimes I closed my eyes. Sometimes I gazed trancelike at the words unspooling in black ink from the retractable tip of my pen. On occasion I would hear the telephone ring or my cell phone vibrate; but these were only distant dispatches from the other side of the veil. When my hand cramped, I soaked it in a basin of warm water and Epsom salt. I drank nothing but bottled spring water and ate only when the hunger cramps in my stomach turned into white-hot conflagrations that threatened to bend me over at the waist.

The notebooks filled up. Outside, the windowsill filled up with snow. Icicles lengthened from the eaves. Icicles shrank and vanished. The snow on the sill turned to water. That pennant of smoke ceased corkscrewing up from my distant neighbor's chimney.

Over my shoulder, the rasping voice of Mr. Cables urged me on, telling me to dance the goodtime dance. If it was night, I would sometimes catch his fleeting trench-coated reflection in the single windowpane—there and then gone, like a haunting. When I slept, I would sometimes come awake to the *clink-clink-clink* of Tony Meeks's wallet-chain chiming against the metal leg of a desk chair.

On the day two police officers showed up on my front porch, I answered the door sporting a full beard and unkempt hair, my right arm wound in kinetic tape. Susan had called them, concerned that I had been unresponsive to her phone calls and emails. I assured the officers I was very much alive. I showed them my driver's license to prove I was who I claimed to be. One of the officers asked me to sign their copy of *Blood Show*, so I did, despite the agony that tore through my hand. When they drove away in their police car, I realized the air was warm and the flowers in my garden were in bloom. Birds sang in the trees and the sky was a clear, dazzling azure. It was spring.

I returned to the den. Prior to the interruption by the police officers, I had written the final sentence of the novel, yet the novel wasn't complete. The *sentence* wasn't complete. It ended just as it had when I first read it in the book, with Mr. Cables as the final commuter on a city bus, printing fastidiously in one of his memo pads. The bus comes to a stop, the doors wheeze open...

And then?

I stood before the desk, twenty pounds lighter than when I'd first began this pilgrimage months earlier, my entire body aching but my mind—my spirit—like a bulb shining brighter, brighter.

I knew the ending.

I sat down, picked up the pen, and wrote it.

17

I SHOWERED, SHAVED, AND got dressed in fresh clothes—something I hadn't done in far too long. I collected all the notebooks, each one filled with lines of prose, and placed them in various cake boxes. Then I stowed the boxes of handwritten manuscript in my basement.

It was a gorgeous afternoon, so I decided to walk instead of drive into town. I carried the hardbound copy of *Mr. Cables* with me. It no longer felt like an intrusion, a heavy burden. I carried it down to the nearest bus stop, where I sat on a bench inside a Plexiglas enclosure. To pass the time, I opened the book and began to read it...but instantly found something about the words on the page to be distasteful. Disquieting. Uncomfortable to the point of being frightening.

I snapped the book closed with an audible pop.

When I heard the metallic keening of brakes, I looked up. A pair of headlights approached over the road. The bus whined to a stop directly in front of me. Its hydraulic doors wheezed open.

Tucking the book under one arm, I got on the bus and headed toward the back, where the figure in the fedora and trench coat sat waiting for me. Aside from the driver, we were the only two people on the bus.

Mr. Cables turned and looked up at me. His face was surprisingly handsome beneath the brim of his fedora. He extended one pale, manicured hand in my direction. I handed him the book, which he placed on the seat beside him. He never took his eyes from me.

"We certainly danced the goodtime dance, didn't we?" he said, and I could see that his teeth were filed into points. "We certainly had a time."

I said nothing; only stared at him.

"A *pleasure*" —the word seethed out of him— "working with you, Mr. Paventeau." He gave me a shark's smile.

"Sir," the driver called from the front of the bus. He was watching me in the elongated rearview mirror above the windshield. "You gotta sit down before I can go."

I looked back at Mr. Cables.

"I believe this is your stop, Quimby," he said to me. He tipped a finger against the brim of his hat.

I let my gaze hang on him a moment longer. Then I turned and headed back toward the front of the bus. I apologized to the driver, who sat there shaking his head in disapproval; then I climbed off the bus. I stood on the curb and watched the hydraulic doors slide shut. A cloud of black diesel belched from the exhaust as the bus pulled away from the curb.

I stared at the man in the fedora, silhouetted in the smoky rear window, until the bus lumbered over the hill and disappeared.

18

I WAS FREE OF Mr. Cables, but I wasn't free of myself.

First thing I did was call Susan. She was relieved to hear my voice then jumped into berating me for disappearing on her like that, and what the hell had I been up to, anyway? I told her it was a very long story, but I was finally in a good place. I told her I would be sending her an email very shortly, and that I wanted the attachment to be included as a preface to the latest edition of *The Body Fields*. She could work out the details with the publisher on my behalf. Even if they didn't like what it said—and they probably wouldn't—I wanted it included in all future editions. If the publisher refused, I'd pull the book and publish it myself.

Susan had questions, of course. I told her to wait for the email. And, in the end, if she decided *she* wanted to distance herself from me, well, I told her I would understand.

"You've been a good agent," I told her, "and a good friend."

"I'm worried about you, Wil."

"The worrying is over. Everything's great now," I told her, and hung up the phone.

Back in the den, I powered up my laptop. Still simmering with the trace vestiges of inspiration, I opened a Word document and typed the words AUTHOR'S NOTE at the top of the page, perfectly centered. I stared at this, turning it over in my head. Then I deleted the word NOTE and replaced it with CONFESSION.

What I wrote was not much different than what I'd told Gloria and Arnold Meeks while sitting in their stuffy living room in their little house in Quimby. It was possibly the most honest thing I'd ever written.

And honest writers, of course, were dangerous writers.

ABOUT THE AUTHOR

(Photo by Debra Malfi)

Ronald Malfi is an award-winning author of several horror novels, mysteries, and thrillers. He is the recipient of two Independent Publisher Book Awards, the Beverly Hills Book Award, the Vincent Preis Horror Award, the Benjamin Franklin Award for Popular Fiction, and his novel *Floating Staircase* was nominated for a Bram Stoker Award®. Most recognized for his haunting, literary style and memorable characters, Malfi's dark fiction has gained acceptance among readers of all genres. He currently lives in Maryland with his wife, Debra, and their two children. When he isn't writing, he's performing with his rock band, VEER.

4/21

CPSIA information can be obtained
at www.ICGtesting.com
Printed in the USA
LVHW051018180421
684828LV00005B/1202